Just the Facts

Alcohol

Pamela G. Richards, M.Ed.

Heinemann Library
Chicago, Illinois

© 2001 Reed Educational & Professional Publishing
Published by Heinemann Library,
an imprint of Reed Educational & Professional Publishing,
100 N. LaSalle, Suite 1010
Chicago, IL 60602
Customer Service 888-454-2279
Visit our website at www.heinemannlibrary.com

Designed by Depke Design
Printed in Hong Kong
05 04 03 02 01
10 9 8 7 6 5 4 3 2 1

Library of Congress Cataloging-in-Publication Data
Richards, Pam, 1966-
    Alcohol / Pam Richards.
        p. cm. -- (Just the facts)
    Includes bibliographical references and index.
    ISBN 1-57572-253-4 (library)
    1. Alcoholism--Juvenile literature. 2. Drinking of alcoholic beverages--Juvenile
literature. 3. Alcoholism--Prevention--Juvenile literature. [1. Alcohol. 2. Alcoholism.]
I. Title. II. Series.

HV5066 .R53 2000
362.292--dc21
                                                        00-
038913

Acknowledgments
The author and publishers are grateful to the following for permission
to reproduce copyright material: P. Baldesare, p. 40; M. Black, p. 15;
G. Boden (inset), p. 4; Bubbles, p. 26; Mary Evans, p. 10; The
Granger Collection, p. 12; Impact, p.8; Index Stock Photography,
Inc., p. 9, 20; Network, p. 7; J. Phillips, p. 46; Photodisc, p. 16, 22,
24, 25, 36, 37, 39, 52, 53, 54, 55, 56; PhotoEdit/Bachmann, p.
11(back), 32; PhotoEdit/J. Boykin, p. 37; PhotoEdit/P. Conklin, p.
48-49; PhotoEdit/G. Conner, p. 11 (inset); PhotoEdit/Mary Kate
Denny, p. 38; PhotoEdit/M. Ferguson, p. 31; PhotoEdit/M. Newman,
p. 17; PhotoEdit/J. Nourok, p. 5; PhotoEdit/A. Ramey, p. 29;
PhototEdit/B. Stitzer, p. 6 (back), 14; PhotoEdit/D. Young-Wolff, p. 4
(back), 7 (inset), 27, 33; PhotoEdit/E. Zuckerman, p. 44 (back);
Photofusion, p. 41, 45; Photo Researchers, p. 21; Science Photo
Library/M. Clarke, p. 23; Science Photo Library/S. Fraser, p. 35;
Stock Boston, p. 19; Stock Boston/M. Burnett, p. 47; Stock
Boston/B. Daemmrich, p. 28; Stock Boston/J. Eastcott/YVA
Momatiuk, p. 13; Stock Boston/S. Grant, p. 50-51 (back); Stock
Boston/Michael Grecco Shayofsky, p. 44 (inset); Tony Stone/Mary
Kate Denny, p. 51 (inset)

Cover photograph: Gareth Boden

About the Author: Pam is a prevention specialist
and educator with over twenty years of experience
in the fields of General Education, Prevention,
Special Education, and Administration. Pam
began working in administration in 1987, first
developing special assessment programs for
young children and later creating the school
system's Drug, Violence, and Character Education
Department. Her expertise in Prevention comes
not only from formal training, but also from
personal experiences. As a result of her own
experience with an alcoholic, Pam understands the
emotional problems that many children bring to
the classroom, and the effects that alcohol use
can have on someone else's life.

> To G. R., my partner in life, and to
> Michael—you truly are a gift from God!

Some words are shown in bold, **like
this.** You can find out what they mean
by looking in the glossary.

Contents

Introduction

Alcohol is a **drug?** No way! When most people think about drugs they think of substances such as cocaine, marijuana, or LSD. To these people, alcohol is "just a drink"–a beverage that tastes good and allows one to "loosen up a bit." The reality, however, is that alcohol is the oldest and most widely used drug in the United States. It can quickly affect the brain's activity and produce long-lasting effects. Nearly half of all Americans over the age of twelve drink alcohol. Although most drink only occasionally, there are an estimated ten to fifteen million alcoholics, or problem drinkers, in the United States. About four and a half million of these alcoholics are adolescents.

> If [alcohol] came in pill form, it would be called a tranquilizer. It would be available by prescription only. The prescription bottle would bear warning labels: "Causes drowsiness—do not take this drug while operating machinery." "Do not use this drug if you are pregnant: Since it effects every system in the body, it would be inadvisable to consume if you have any health concerns, especially diabetes, liver, or heart disease." You would be a given only a small supply at a time. You would be cautioned to watch for potentially serious side effects, and advised to discontinue its use if you experienced any. Your dosage would be carefully monitored, and you would be watched for signs of abuse or addition.
>
> -1994 Duke University

Alcohol and crime

Studies show that alcohol use is involved in one-half of all murders, accidental deaths, and suicides; one-third of all drowning, boating, and aviation deaths; one-half of all crimes; and almost half of all fatal automobile accidents. The U.S. Department of Justice found that alcohol abuse was a factor in 40 percent of the violent crimes committed in the United States.

A potent drug

Alcohol produces changes in brain activities. These changes seem pleasurable in small amounts because they build one's confidence and relaxation levels. But if alcohol is abused, these changes become dangerous, and can destroy a person's brain and body. Alcohol can destroy families. It can destroy love, trust, respect, and friendship. It makes people act unpredictably. It makes other family members angry and ashamed. It causes neurological, cardiological, and respiratory problems that may result in permanent injury, or even death.

Alcohol's attraction

There are a number of reasons why alcohol is tolerated. It is socially acceptable. Its consumption is a part of many social gatherings—weddings, birthday celebrations, and formal receptions. In the United States, alcohol is legal if you are over the age of 21, but most people under 21 have no trouble getting it either. Alcohol is often tolerated as a rite of passage, a sign of adulthood. Alcohol **addiction** develops slowly for most people. Although it appears to develop more rapidly in young people, the gradual onset of the disease often makes it difficult to notice. Even a severely addicted person often does not know what has happened.

Costs related to alcohol abuse

Recent data indicates that alcohol and **alcoholism** cost society an estimated $166.5 billion in 1995. This reflects a cost of one and one-half times that attributed to **drug** abuse and dependence. This money is spent on health care costs, premature deaths, impaired productivity, motor vehicle crashes, and costs of crime attributed to alcohol abuse.

An unknown risk

Alcohol affects individuals differently. Genetics, gender, and body weight and type all play an important part on how alcohol is absorbed. A person doesn't know what will happen until he or she has taken that first drink. By then, it may be too late. Is it a risk that you are willing to take? Reading this book and understanding the possible consequences will help you make educated decisions about alcohol.

What is Alcohol?

Alcohol is a **drug.** It's a **depressant,** or sedative drug, that slows down the functions of the **central nervous system.** It affects people's immediate behavior and can cause lasting effects if it is consumed in large quantities over a period of time. Alcohol is a general term that describes a family of organic chemicals with common properties. Members of this family include **ethanol,** or ethyl alcohol, methanol, isopropanol, and others. The most commonly ingested form of alcohol is ethanol.

Ethanol is a clear, unstable liquid that burns easily. It is made up of carbon, oxygen, and hydrogen. Its chemical formula is C_2H_5OH. If you remove the water from the ethanol, you get ether. Ether is an anesthetic that affects the brain and puts it to sleep. Ethanol has a slight characteristic odor and is very water-soluble. Because of this water-solubility, alcohol is quickly absorbed into the bloodstream and then distributed throughout the body. Even in small amounts, alcohol can affect the central nervous system because it is distributed so quickly and thoroughly.

The distillation process converts grains and fruits into alcohol.

It is the brain that is affected first, which is why some people act or talk more freely than they would if they had not ingested alcohol. This initial relaxation or loss of **inhibition** is what often attracts people to drink alcohol. However, as the **blood alcohol content,** or BAC, increases, a person's response to stimuli decreases, having a harmful effect on judgment, coordination, and reaction time. Drinking too much alcohol in a short period of time can lead to alcohol poisoning, which can be fatal. Ethanol is produced using various processes. Wines and beers are produced through **fermentation** or brewing. In fermentation, some of the sugar in fruit juice or a grain solution gradually turns into alcohol. Hard liquor, or spirits, is produced through a special chemical process known as **distillation**. Distillation produces higher concentrations of alcohol than can be created through fermentation.

Products containing alcohol

Common beverages containing alcohol include wine, beer, wine coolers, brandy, scotch, gin, rum, and whiskey. A 12-ounce can of beer, a 5-ounce glass of wine, and 1.5 ounces of 80 proof liquor contain the same amount of ethanol—about .6 ounces. Some medications and foods have small amounts of alcohol in them as well.

A standard drink is:

- One 12-ounce (355 mL) bottle of beer or wine cooler
- One 5-ounce (148 mL) glass of wine
- 1.5 ounces (44 mL) of an 80-proof distilled spirit

History of Alcohol

Alcoholic beverages date back many thousands of years and appear in the written records of the earliest civilizations. Grapes grow in many regions of the Middle East, and early citizens there noted that grape juice would ferment to become wine. Archaeologists have suggested that the first cultivated vineyards were developed in the Caucasus region, near present-day Georgia and Armenia, between 6,000 and 4,000 B.C. Grape cultivation and **fermentation,** as well as beer brewing, spread throughout the Middle East and became firmly established in the societies of ancient Mesopotamia and Egypt.

Setting the pattern

The ancient Greeks fermented their wines in resin-coated vats and then filtered the wines into clay storage vessels for export. This started the alcohol industry, and influenced the Romans, who followed the Greek example. The Romans planted vineyards across their empire wherever the soil and climate were favorable.

The fall of the Roman Empire in the fifth century A.D. temporarily ended the popularity of wine. Europeans still produced wine, but the quality declined and most of it was used for religious purposes. Beers also remained popular. The biggest development in the history of alcohol was **distillation**. The distillation process concentrates the amount of alcohol in a liquid while removing many of the unpleasant tastes. Although it had been done for many years in East Asia, Arabs brought distilling to the Middle East and Europe relatively late. By the eleventh century, Europeans had learned the technique, and the Irish, followed by the Scots, produced the first whiskies by distilling grains.

As the Middle Ages gave way to the Renaissance, present-day drinking patterns in Europe had been established. Good quality wine was once more available from southern countries, while northern Europeans had mastered the art of producing beers and ales. Eastern Europeans distilled and drank vodka. Pubs, beer cellars, taverns, and inns sold these drinks, which were now deeply woven into the social fabric of most cultures.

In the eighteenth century, a great change occurred when gin was introduced to Britain. Gin is liquor like whiskey or vodka, but at that time it was far easier and cheaper to produce, and it required no aging before drinking it. As a result, gin supplies were huge, and the level of drunkenness soared. By the beginning of the nineteenth century, Britain had enacted laws to control widespread drinking. One such law, The Gin Act, raised the cost of that liquor. Another law aimed to ban youth from pubs. Religious leaders and citizens against alcohol led this **Temperance Movement**, which was also active in the United States.

Concerned about the effects that alcohol was having on soldiers and workers in ammunition factories during World War I, the British government passed strict drinking laws. Soon after the war, the United States also took more drastic action in order to control alcohol. In 1919, leaders in the Temperance Movement achieved their goal when the Eighteenth Amendment to the Constitution made it illegal to sell alcohol or to transport it for sale. Government leaders believed that banning alcohol would reduce the number of drunk and unemployed, and reduce crime rates. Indeed, obvious changes in criminal activity occurred. Americans found that a great deal of money could be made by smuggling and selling alcohol. **Bootleggers** were able to make as much as an 800 percent profit. Even the average citizen began rum running and consuming alcohol. For the first time, many Americans were proudly committing crimes against their country. Government officials were known to throw parties with alcoholic beverages. Prohibition agents and police officers were often bribed to ignore the illegal sale of alcohol. Some of them were involved in rum running and bootlegging. The **National Prohibition**

Act lasted until 1933, when it was repealed by the Twenty-first Amendment. Since Prohibition ended, public policymakers have continued to struggle with the issues surrounding the alcohol problem. People drink alcoholic beverages at many kinds of occasions—most in social surroundings. Not all people abuse alcohol, but the ones who do can be dangerous to themselves and others. Governments have the difficult job of allowing responsible people to enjoy alcohol at social events while at the same time keeping highways, neighborhoods, and citizens safe from people who abuse it. Today most prevention approaches focus on youth education and mass public-awareness campaigns.

FRIENDS DON'T LET FRIENDS DRIVE DRUNK

Why People Drink

Why do people drink alcohol? Most people don't drink to get drunk, but merely to "feel good and have fun." Sometimes religious or cultural traditions include the use of alcohol in a ceremony or celebration. Many people accept that teens will experiment with alcohol at some point. Unfortunately, many adolescents' abuse or dependence on alcohol begins with experimentation. Why do people choose to drink? There is no one answer, but studies have shown that most people drink for the following reasons.

Social acceptance

Nobody likes to feel ill at ease at a party. Everybody likes to have fun. Drinking in order to be one of the crowd is a reason given frequently by young people and those over the age of 21. Everyone wants to feel accepted by his or her peers. Drinking to strengthen a weak self-image is not unusual, either. Whether a lack of positive self-esteem is the result of a traumatic childhood experience, school or work failure, or a broken relationship, alcohol looks like the answer to many people. However, once the initial feeling of **euphoria** from the alcohol fades, drinking to cope with or to escape from unwanted feelings or a poor sense of self usually will result in worse feelings and thoughts. Feeling sad or depressed after a drinking episode often leads to feelings of guilt, which then can lead to more drinking. It's an overwhelming cycle for most people. College students and adults may drink just to get "high." The desire to have a good time overrides these groups' intellectual awareness that alcohol has the potential for great harm.

But alcohol is very easy to get or buy. Many stadiums and citywide celebrations sell alcohol to adults, and alcohol is served at various social functions in America, such as weddings and business receptions. There are also people who drink purely because they enjoy the taste of the alcoholic beverage.

Young people begin using alcohol for an assortment of reasons. Just like adults, kids are often trying to forget their problems, and drink to cope with a range of feelings. Adolescents are eager to feel like one of the crowd, and to be accepted by their peers. The desire for popularity is particularly strong in this age group. The adolescent years can be very difficult years to experience. It is natural for most teenagers to try to assert their independence by trying to act like adults. Growing up quickly is important to them, and modeling adult behavior, such as drinking, in order to feel better or to cover up feelings of rejection is one way to feel grown up.

Is peer pressure real?

Many studies link young adults' drinking to peer pressure. Yet the "everybody's doing it" reasoning doesn't hold true in all situations. The responses in an alcohol and drug survey administered to fifth through twelfth graders in one Tennessee school district revealed that the perceived number of peers thought to being drinking alcohol or using other **drugs** was significantly higher than the actual number of students who used these substances.

Another reason young people want to drink is to appear more grown up. They might think drinking is more mature, since they see adults doing it. In fact, it is more mature for a young person to turn down a drink, because:

1) Alcohol is an illegal drug for anyone under 21;

2) Drinking alcohol is an enormous health risk to the developing body of an adolescent;

3) Young people are at much greater risk to use other drugs if they begin drinking;

4) Adolescents who use alcohol are more likely to be aggressive, skip school, run away from home, and feel depressed. They are also more likely to show delinquent and criminal behaviors, be involved in theft, and try to hurt themselves or others.

The alcohol beverage industry spends one billion dollars annually to pay for advertisements and lobbying. It also supports some political issues and nonprofit causes. This makes people feel that the alcohol industry is helping their community. Most alcohol companies set aside a large amount of money to use for helping people who have alcohol problems, or for educating people about using alcohol responsibly. The support of community programming against alcohol and other drug abuse is new for some manufacturers, while others have supported and funded various drug prevention programs for years. However, many foundations and groups that receive funding from the alcohol industry are hesitant to support policies or laws that would hurt the industry's profits. So, is the alcohol industry really supporting prevention efforts, or are they simply using them as a tactic to maintain the support of the American people?

Manufacturers of alcoholic beverages market their products in a variety of ways. Although they often reject the claim that they are "marketing to America's youth," the manufactures can't refute their use of child-friendly cartoon characters in their ads, nor can they refute that television ads will reach millions of American children, even if they are only aired late at night.

Media impact

Studies show that people's decisions to use alcohol and other **drugs** are influenced by exposure to pro-use messages in the mass media. Hundreds of millions of dollars worth of beer and wine commercials, and most recently liquor ads, glamorize and glorify drinking. Ads focus heavily on promoting one beverage or brand over another in order to entice drinkers toward a product. Alcohol advertising especially affects young people's developing beliefs about drinking. Students have reported that television commercials lead them to view drinking as normal. The effects of frequent

> **Television advertising for alcoholic beverages affects the manner, style, and meanings of drinking in society. It defines drinking as a positive and normative behavior. The ubiquity of the ads promotes an exaggerated view of the degree of alcohol used in socity. Kids learn how, where, when, and why to drink from the ads.**
>
> — Center for Science in the Public Interest

exposure to television beer ads include a child's ability to recognize and recall brand names, the ability to match brand names and beer slogans, the establishment of values relating beer to party times and fun, and an expectation of drinking as an adult.

The media has a significant effect on increasing boys' and older adolescents' drinking habits, since this audience is exposed to more alcohol ads. In addition to advertisements, television shows often include drinking scenes. Before reaching the age of 18, the average child will see more than 75,000 drinking scenes on TV. Radio and print ads can be just as harmful to developing minds. Ads are often placed on rock stations and in magazines that target college audiences, but many younger adolescents listen to these stations and read these magazines as well. The advertisements they hear and see teach them that drinking is a normal part of having fun.

What Happens When You Drink?

You may decide to drink, or you may decide not to. Your family values, your religious beliefs, your choice of friends, and your community's attitude towards teenage drinking will likely affect your choice. You also need to consider what takes place when a person decides to ingest alcohol. What changes occur behaviorally, emotionally, physically, and socially? Do your relationships with your family and friends change? What about your schoolwork? What about legal consequences? Are the effects immediate? What happens if you continue to drink over a long period of time?

Drinking can do great damage to your liver, the organ that breaks down the alcohol.

Many factors affect what happens when a person consumes alcohol. Gender, size, weight, physical condition, food intake, and the rate of alcohol consumption all determine the effect that alcohol has on the body. Women tend to achieve a higher **blood alcohol content** due, in part, to their greater percentage of body fat. If all other variables are the same, and a man and a woman both ingest the same amount of alcohol, the woman will tend to reach a higher blood alcohol content level. The effect is even quicker on children and young adults because their bodies are not fully developed. Their livers are still developing and are unable to process ethyl alcohol as quickly as an adult's. Greater poisoning can occur when a young person drinks, because only five percent of the alcohol consumed is eliminated from the body. The remaining 95 percent is oxidized, or broken down, by the liver. This means that a young person gets **intoxicated** much faster than an adult does.

What Happens When You Drink?
Short-term Effects

Short-term behavioral changes

Initially, alcohol can make a person feel terrific. Alcohol is a depressant drug, so it relaxes the person. It can actually lower inhibitions and make a person feel as though he or she can accomplish anything. This feeling of relaxation may feel good at first, but is likely to cause unpredictable behavior and uncontrollable emotions. Drinking may cause some people to take sexual risks and behave in ways that they would not normally. Unwanted pregnancy and sexually transmitted diseases often occur as the results of excessive drinking. Alcohol may make a person feel like he or she is performing better, but at the same time that it relaxes, alcohol has a damaging effect on judgment, coordination, and reaction time. Other immediate behavioral effects include slurred speech, talkativeness, sudden mood changes, and violent behavior.

Short-term physiological effects

The direct effects of alcohol on the body's organs and systems are numerous. Within moments of ingestion, alcohol reaches the brain. This immediate attack on the **central nervous system**, the body's "computer," slows down brain activity and may cause dizziness, difficulty with motor skills, disturbed sleep, impaired learning, nausea, and vomiting. Diarrhea and gastritis, an inflammation of the stomach lining, may also occur. These latter effects are related to the alcohol's attack on the stomach lining itself. Alcohol gets in the way of messages going to your brain and changes your perceptions and emotions, vision, hearing, and coordination. If enough alcohol is consumed to raise the **blood alcohol content** level to 0.10 percent—a level of legal intoxication in all states—then the following short-term physiological effects may happen: loss of physical coordination, loss of balance, incoherent speech, slowed thinking, confusion, and impaired short-term memory.

Even small amounts of alcohol can have damaging effects. Recently, researchers have discovered that no more than one or two drinks a week will promote aging. So if you want to have clear skin and bright eyes, don't drink. Alcohol can ruin your good looks, give you bad breath, and make you gain weight.

Short-term psychological or emotional effects

People often find the initial short-term effects of alcohol pleasurable. Feelings of great self-confidence and ability are often an immediate effect of drinking alcohol. But this "I can do anything," feeling usually doesn't last long, particularly if alcohol continues to be consumed. An individual may drink because he or she is depressed, but because alcohol is a depressant, it will actually bring the person down even

more, and may cause feelings of despair and hopelessness. In the long run, the effects of alcohol use can be negative and costly. Not only does the body physically sustain injury from the use of alcohol, regular use may cause a psychological or emotional dependence. A person may feel the need to always "take a drink" prior to a certain type of situation—perhaps before a test in school, before going on a date, or before talking to the boss at work. Relying on alcohol to feel good is a dangerous dependence on alcohol. It can easily lead to greater and more frequent use of alcohol or other drugs just to make it through a normal day. This dependence is sometimes referred to a craving, since the person needs alcohol's psychological effects, even though the actual amount of alcohol is not necessarily enough to produce serious levels of intoxication.

Short-term effects on family and friends

Friends and family members may be embarrassed or even frightened by the actions and behavior of a person drinking alcohol. If an adolescent causes damage to property or to another person while under the influence of alcohol, his or her family may be held responsible. Since drinking can cause serious injury or even death, the decision to drink may have a powerful negative effect on family and friends. This is particularly true when drinking and driving are mixed. Good friends can be injured or killed by one person's decision to drink and drive!

Short-term educational impact

Many students don't realize that the alcohol consumed over the weekend may have a profound effect two or three days later. Young people who drink on the weekend are neither physically nor psychologically prepared to learn and perform on Monday morning. Students who drink frequently often fail tests, reduce their classroom participation, and leave their homework incomplete, if they attempt it at all.

Immediate legal issues

Many states have passed legislation that delays or suspends the driving privileges of juveniles caught drinking, buying, or possessing alcohol. Increases in car insurance rates are one deterrent. Also, young people may lose their driver's licenses for an entire year if they are caught drinking or in possession of alcoholic beverages. Some states even go so far as attaching ignition interlocks to vehicles in order to prevent offenders from driving.

Death of an Innocent

I went to a party, Mom; I remembered what you said.
You told me not to drink, Mom, so I drank soda instead.
I really felt proud inside, Mom, the way you said I would.
I didn't drink and drive, Mom, even though the others said I should.

I know I did the right thinking, Mom, I know you are always right.
Now the party is finally ending, Mom, as everyone is driving out of sight.
As I got into my car, Mom, I knew I'd get home in one piece
Because of the way you raised me, so responsible and sweet.

I started to drive away, Mom, but as I pulled out into the road,
The other car didn't see me, Mom, and hit me like a load.
As I lay there on the pavement, Mom, I hear the policeman say,
The other guy is drunk, Mom, and now I'm the one who will pay.

I'm lying here dying, Mom... I wish you'd get here soon.
How could this happen to me, Mom? My life just burst like a balloon.
There is blood all around, Mom, and most of it is mine.
I hear the medic say, Mom, I'll die in a short time.

I just wanted to tell you, Mom, I swear I didn't drink.
It was the others, Mom. The others didn't think.
He was probably at the same party as I.
The only difference is, he drank, and I will die.

Why do people drink, Mom? It can ruin your whole life.
I'm feeling sharp pains now. Pains just like a knife.
The guy who hit me is wailing, Mom, and I don't think it's fair.
I'm lying here dying and all he can do is stare.

Tell my brother not to cry, Mom. Tell Daddy to be brave.
And when I go to heaven, Mom, put "Daddy's Girl" on my grave.
Someone should have told him, Mom, not to drink and drive.
If only they had told him, Mom, I would still be alive.

My breath is getting shorter, Mom. I'm becoming very scared.
Please don't cry for me, Mom. When I needed you, you were always there.
I have only one last question, Mom, before I say good-bye.
I didn't drink and drive, so why am I the one to die?

                              -Anonymous

What Happens When You Drink?
Long-term Effects

Long-term use or abuse of alcohol may lead to **alcoholism** a progressive and potentially fatal disease. It can also cause other health problems, which may take years to develop, but can significantly reduce the life expectancy and quality of life of an individual. Continuing to drink despite the onset of health problems is a clear sign that a person is abusing alcohol. In addition to deteriorating health, risk of injury or fatal accidents increases with continued alcohol use.

Loss of friends can be a result of long-term alcohol abuse.

Fetal Alcohol Syndrome is linked to heavy drinking during pregnancy.

Long-term behavioral changes

Usually, the longer one continues to drink, the less he or she cares about appearance. Grooming habits may go unchecked, and diet may be ignored. Irritability, violent outbursts, and severe mood changes are often behavioral symptoms of continued drinking. Memory loss can be significant.

Long-term physiological effects

Many poor health conditions can be attributed to long-time alcohol use. Vitamin deficiencies, elevated blood pressure and heart rate, risk of stroke and heart failure, stomach ailments, skin problems, sexual impotence, and severe liver damage are likely to occur. Painful things like stomach ulcers, and pancreatitis, an extremely painful inflammation of the pancreas, chronic diarrhea, mouth and throat cancer, and respiratory disorders like pneumonia and tuberculosis, are likely results of unrelenting and abusive alcohol use. Even drinking just one drink per day may increase the risk of breast cancer in a woman. Vision, circulation, fertility, and decreased immunity are also possibilities.

Fetal Alcohol Syndrome (FAS) is a term associated with irreversible birth anomalies attributed to heavy drinking during pregnancy. In a pregnant woman, alcohol actually passes from the mother to the unborn child through the placenta. The **central nervous system** of the **fetus** is severely depressed. Since the liver is unable to process the toxic alcohol, the substance remains in the body of the fetus for a very long period of time, and the unborn child is **intoxicated.**

Long-term psychological or emotional effects

Psychological effects of alcohol abuse include increased moments of anger and mood swings, drinking alone, anxiety, and depression. Violent outbursts, even toward loved ones, are not uncommon. Thoughts of suicide are common as feelings of loneliness and despair take over in a person's mind.

Long-term effects on family and friends

Recurrent arguments or fighting with family members or friends is likely. Parents are often so troubled by a child's continual drinking habits that they are forced to use "tough love" tactics, such as asking a child to move out of the home. Old friends tend to stay away, unless they too are on the alcohol abuse pathway.

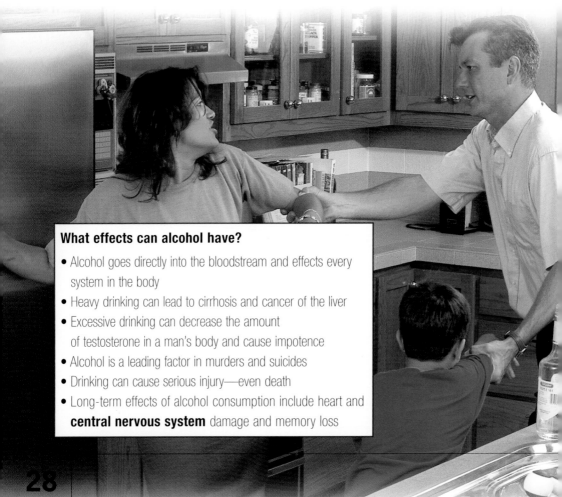

What effects can alcohol have?

- Alcohol goes directly into the bloodstream and effects every system in the body
- Heavy drinking can lead to cirrhosis and cancer of the liver
- Excessive drinking can decrease the amount of testosterone in a man's body and cause impotence
- Alcohol is a leading factor in murders and suicides
- Drinking can cause serious injury—even death
- Long-term effects of alcohol consumption include heart and **central nervous system** damage and memory loss

Long-term educational impact

Failing grades, loss of credit, and rejections from colleges or technical schools are all possible and likely to occur with long-term alcohol abuse. If a student is caught drinking alcohol at school or at a school function, most schools in the country will suspend him or her, sometimes for as long as one full academic year.

Legal issues

Detentions in juvenile hall, community service, or imprisonment are just a few of the consequences one might experience if drinking gets out of control. In a few states, a driver's license is confiscated immediately upon arrest for a DWI, or driving while intoxicated. It is returned if the person is found not guilty. However, the person remains without a driver's license until such a time. More and more states are demanding prison terms for people found guilty of causing an accident while under the influence of alcohol.

Should you drink?

The decision to use alcohol, even occasionally, is not an easy decision to make. Although your family values and standards play an integral part in your decision, so do the opinions and actions of your peers. Remember that using alcohol at an early age may lead to using other **drugs** later. You may think that you are only experimenting, but do you know that you will be able to stop drinking if something bad happens?

Alcoholism

What is Alcoholism?

Alcoholism is an illness. Though it was once looked upon as a moral problem, today most people realize that **addiction** to alcohol is a **chemical dependency** on the **drug** that can be treated. According to the National Council on Alcoholism and Drug Dependence,

Alcoholism is a primary, chronic disease with genetic, psychosocial, and environmental factors, which influence its development and manifestations. The disease is progressive and fatal, and is characterized by continuous or periodic impaired control over drinking, a preoccupation with alcohol, the use of alcohol despite negative consequences, and distortions in thinking, most notably denial.

There is no cure for alcoholism, but it is treatable. With proper treatment, alcoholics can lead full and satisfying lives. Alcoholics cannot always stop at just one or two drinks. They may start out with the same intentions as a nonalcoholic, but they are unable to control the urge to drink more. Drinking becomes a compulsion, and alcoholics become victims to this compulsion. Oddly, alcoholics may remain dry, or alcohol-free, for weeks or even months. Once they do drink again, however, they lose control of their actions—the urge to drink is so strong that they cannot stop. Preoccupation with drinking, denial, and continued drinking in spite of knowing the potential dangers are all common behaviors of a person with alcoholism. Close friends or family members will often try to hide the alcohol or distract the person from drinking. But it's impossible to keep an alcoholic away from alcohol.

Alcoholism can be almost invisible as it develops. After continued exposure to alcohol, the brain begins to adapt to the changes that alcohol makes in the centers responsible for pleasure sensations. The brain becomes dependent on the alcohol in order to stimulate feelings of pleasure. Some alcoholics develop a **tolerance** to the

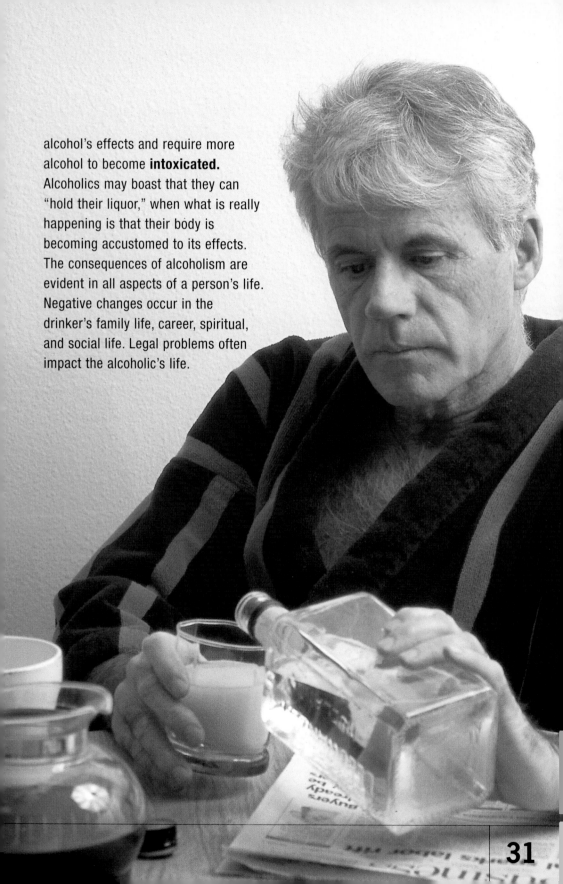

alcohol's effects and require more alcohol to become **intoxicated.** Alcoholics may boast that they can "hold their liquor," when what is really happening is that their body is becoming accustomed to its effects. The consequences of alcoholism are evident in all aspects of a person's life. Negative changes occur in the drinker's family life, career, spiritual, and social life. Legal problems often impact the alcoholic's life.

Beginning stages of alcoholism

Alcoholics develop the disease in many different ways. Some alcoholics drink to the point of **intoxication** from their first drink. They immediately show behavior destructive to their health and their interpersonal relationships. Others develop the disease at a much slower and progressive pace. However, the alcoholic comes to depend upon the alcohol to make it through life events. Whether celebrating, mourning, socializing, or for some reason in need of a "perk up," the alcoholic craves the mood-altering characteristics of alcohol. As the disease progresses, alcoholics don't need a specific reason to drink, and they certainly prefer social events where alcohol is available. Alcoholics feel uncomfortable at parties or occasions where alcohol is absent. Friends who drink are preferred over nondrinkers. The compulsion to begin drinking usually begins earlier in the day. **Tolerance** for alcohol increases, but so does the lack of control, and the frequency of drunkenness. Although an alcoholic may not always get drunk, more and more episodes of drunkenness will take place as the disease progresses. A type of amnesia, referred to as a black out, may occur. It's even possible that an alcoholic will have more than one **black out** within a single drinking period. Evidence actually exists that certain doctors, who were alcoholics, are known to have performed major surgical operations during such a black out. They did not remember performing the surgery later.

During the middle stages, the alcoholic may become worried and embarrassed, or ashamed about his or her lack of control over drinking. Different strategies may be attempted to control or stop the drinking: changing to a different alcoholic beverage, moving to a new city or job, or changing brands of alcohol. These attempts are rarely successful, and often lead to the alcoholic's **denial** of a drinking problem. Denial allows the drinker to ignore any feelings of worry or guilt, and continue drinking. Everyone and everything other than the alcohol is blamed for the mounting problems in the alcoholic's life. Conflicts in relationships, both personal and work-related, often lead to anger, violence, and self-hatred.

Final stages

Despite the anger, self-pity, possible loss of employment, or even imprisonment, the alcoholic keeps drinking. Nothing and no one will get in the way of the obsession with alcohol, and the compulsion to drink. Although the alcoholic continues to feel guilty and fearful of crowds and public places, nothing stops the drinking. Late stage **alcoholism** is characterized by cirrhosis of the liver and severe withdrawal symptoms when alcohol is withheld. Unless an alcoholic receives hospitalization or some other sort of therapy, the final stages of alcoholism are insanity and death.

What Causes Alcoholism?

Although a great deal of research has been done on the causes of **alcoholism** the subject is complicated. Genetics, physical and emotional factors, and family structures all play a role in whether a person will develop the disease. In addition, daily life situations play an important part in influencing whether a person develops alcoholism. People with a family history of alcoholism have a far greater risk of developing the disease. Researchers now believe that alcoholism can be an inherited disease, passed down through generations. A child of an alcoholic has four times the risk of becoming an alcoholic than a child of nonalcoholic parents. However, anyone who begins drinking before the age of twenty has a greater risk of developing the disease. Other **risk factors** include having older brothers or sisters who use **drugs,** living in a family where violence is present, and living in a home with poor or inconsistent parenting. **Ethnicity** also affects alcoholic risk. Irish and Native Americans are at increased risk for alcoholism, while Asian and Jewish Americans' risks are decreased. Emotional disorders, such as prolonged depression, anxiety, and personality traits such as impulsiveness or novelty-seeking behavior, also seem to place people at higher risk for alcoholism.

Medical problems

The liver is the organ most affected by alcoholism. A high incidence of alcoholic hepatitis, an inflammation of the liver, and a scarring of the liver, called cirrhosis, occur among chronic alcohol abusers. Symptoms of cirrhosis are not apparent until great damage has been done. Other medical conditions resulting from alcoholism are brain damage, mental disorders, heart disease, cancer, gastrointestinal problems, pneumonia, skin, muscle, and bone disorders, hypoglycemia, or low blood sugar, malnutrition, and a severe Vitamin B deficiency known as Wernicke-Korsakoff syndrome. Symptoms of Wernicke-Korsakoff syndrome include loss of balance, confusion, and memory loss. Eventually the syndrome can result in permanent brain damage and death.

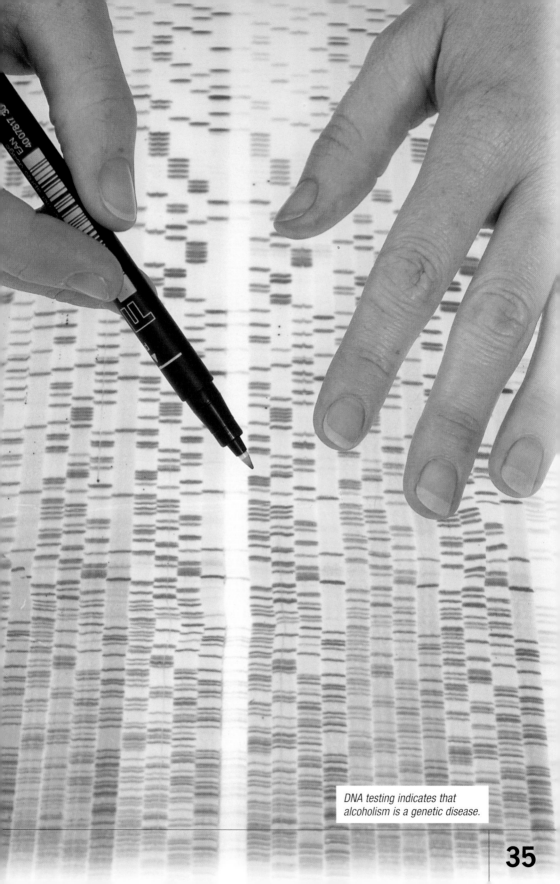

DNA testing indicates that
alcoholism is a genetic disease.

Treatment and Recovery

Various approaches to treating **alcoholism** are available. Some people begin their **recovery** in a hospital setting, while others talk with private psychologists or social workers experienced in working with **alcoholics** and their families. Others attend private clinics that specialize in treating alcoholism. Regardless of the setting, treatment will introduce the principles of recovery. The disease of **chemical dependency** or **addiction** will be covered, as well as instruction on the survival skills necessary to stay sober. Recovery involves treating the whole person and addresses physical, behavioral, emotional, spiritual, sexual, and mental issues. Families and friends will be included in the recovery process because the disease affects the people closest to the alcoholic as well. They must learn about their role in the recovery process and take responsibility for their own actions, not balme themselves for those of the alcoholic. Adolescents in treatment have special issues and needs that must be addressed in their recovery program. Peer pressure, dependency on parents, school issues, and developmental issues such as unrealistic expectations, impulsiveness, loneliness, and separation are all examined. Any good treatment program for adults or teenage alcoholics also involves regular attendance at Alcoholics Anonymous, or AA, meetings.

Alcoholics Anonymous

Alcoholics Anonymous is a fellowship of men and women who share their experiences, strength, and hope with each other in order to solve their common problem and help others recover from alcoholism. No professional counselor facilitates the group. The members themselves, united by their common problems with alcohol, take turns leading the meetings. Men, women, and young people form the membership. Many different social, economic, and cultural backgrounds are represented in the membership. AA groups are in many cities and rural areas throughout the world. Many groups are listed in local telephone directories.

The Twelve Steps of Alcoholics Anonymous

1. We admitted we were powerless over alcohol—that our lives had become unmanageable
2. Came to believe that a Power greater than ourselves could restore us to sanity.
3. Made a decision to turn our will and our lives over to the care of God, as we understood Him.
4. Made a searching and fearless moral inventory of ourselves.
5. Admitted to God, to ourselves, and to another human being the exact nature of our wrongs.
6. Were entirely ready to have God remove all these defects of character.
7. Humbly asked Him to remove our shortcomings.
8. Made a list of all persons we harmed, and became willing to make amends to them all.
9. Made direct amends to such people wherever possible, except when to do so would injure them or others.
10 Continued to take personal inventory and when we were wrong promptly admitted it.
11. Sought through prayer and meditation to improve our conscious contact with God, as we understood Him, praying only for knowledge of His will for us and the power to carry that out.
12. Having a spiritual awakening as the result of these steps, we tried to carry this message to alcoholics, and to practice these principles in all our affairs.

Children of Alcoholics

Due to genetics playing a major role in the development of **alcoholism,** sons and daughters of alcoholic parents are much more likely to develop the disease. Early on, children of **alcoholics** learn to keep the alcoholism a secret from friends, teachers, relatives, or other adults. Often, the child sees himself or herself as the main cause of the alcoholic parent's drinking. Fearful of embarrassment, the children shy away from inviting friends into the home. Because of repeated disappointment with the drinking parent, trust is difficult for children of alcoholics, and this carries into their adult relationships. Anger and depression are common feelings, as is a sense of hopelessness. These children have lower self-esteem throughout childhood, adolescence, and adulthood. Living in an alcoholic home destroys the sense of normalcy children need in order to grow into healthy and well-adjusted members of society. Help is available through twelve-step support groups similar to Alcoholics Anonymous.

Fetal Alcohol Syndrome

Even moderate amounts of alcohol can have irreversible physical and mental damage to a growing **fetus**. Consuming alcohol during pregnancy is dangerous, unnecessary, and unfair to the unborn child. Any female who could be pregnant owes it to her child not to drink at any time during pregnancy. Symptoms of **Fetal Alcohol Syndrome,** or FAS, include severe mental retardation due to impaired brain development, **central nervous system** problems, small size, low birth weight or growth retardation, and facial or skull abnormalities. Children with Fetal Alcohol Syndrome experience great difficulty learning. They are often hyperactive, impulsive, and easily distracted. They may also show problems with comprehension, judgment, critical thinking skills, and processing sensory information. Children with FAS are at a higher risk of developing alcohol and other **drug addictions.**

Youth and Alcohol

Current trends in alcohol use

The costs of underage drinking in the United States total more than $59 billion annually. Alcohol is the number one **drug** of choice among our nation's youth, and it is costing society an average of $600 per year for every United States household. These results, from the study Underage Drinking: Immediate Consequences and their Costs, were developed through a grant from the Office of Juvenile Justice and Delinquency Prevention (OJJDP). This study also broke down the annual costs of alcohol use by youth as follows:

Traffic crashes $18,200,000,000
Violent crime $36,400,000,000
Burns $459,000,000
Drownings $771,000,000

Suicide attempts $1,510,000,000
Fetal Alcohol Syndrome $493,000,000
Alcohol poisonings $948,000,000
Treatment $1,008,000,000

What are the facts?

- Alcohol kills more teenagers than all other drugs combined (CDC, 1995).
- 82 percent of high school seniors have used alcohol; in comparison 65 percent have smoked cigarettes; 50 percent have used marijuana; and 9 percent have used cocaine (1997 Monitoring the Future Survey).
- Young people illegally consume almost 3.6 billion drinks annually, or 10 million drinks each day (US Department of Health, and Human Services, 1998).
- More than half of all eighth graders and 8 of 10 twelfth graders report having tried alcohol (1998 Monitoring the Future Survey).
- Purchase and public possession of alcohol by people under the age of 21 is illegal in all 50 states (US Department of Health and Human Services, 1991).
- Approximately two-thirds of teenagers who drink report that they can buy their own alcoholic beverages (US Department of Health and Human Services, 1991).
- People who begin drinking before age 15 are 4 times more likely to develop **alcoholism** than those who begin at 21 (National Institute on Alcohol Abuse and Alcoholism, 1998).
- Approximately 8 percent of the nation's eighth graders; 22 percent of tenth graders; and 34 percent of twelfth graders have been drunk during the last month (National Institute Drug Abuse, 1997).
- Alcohol is a factor in the three leading causes of death among 15 to 24 year olds: accidents, homicides and suicides (CDC, 1995).
- 56 percent of students in grades five to twelve say that alcohol advertising encourages them to drink (The Scholastic/CNN Newsroom Survey on Student Attitudes About Drug and Substance Abuse, 1990).
- Researchers estimate that alcohol use is implicated in one to two thirds of sexual assault and acquaintance, or date rape, cases among teens and college students (Department of Health and Human Services, 1992).
- Drivers under the age of 25 were more likely than those 25 or older to be intoxicated in a fatal crash (CDC, 1991).
- Junior/middle and senior high school students drink 35 percent of all wine coolers sold in the United States; they also consume 1.1 billion cans of beer (Department of Health and Human Services).

Tracking pattern of alcohol usage

National research is conducted annually in order to determine alcohol and other **drug** usage patterns in America. Two studies, the Monitoring the Future Study, conducted by the Institute for Social Research at the University of Michigan, and the National Household Survey on Drug Abuse, sponsored by the federal Substance Abuse and Mental Health Services Administration (SAMHSA), are the primary sources of statistical information on the use of illegal drugs.

1999 Monitoring the Future Survey results

Since it began, this study has been supported by research grants from the National Institute of Drug Abuse, a division of the U.S. Department of Health and Human Services. The study began in 1975 with a survey of high school seniors. Surveys of eighth and tenth grade students were added in 1991. At each grade level, students are selected to be representative of all students in public and

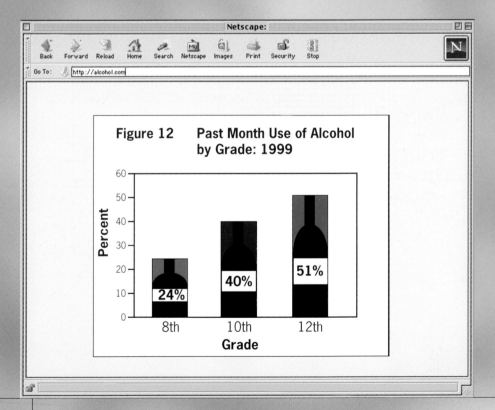

Figure 12   Past Month Use of Alcohol by Grade: 1999

private schools in the United States. The survey is completely self-administered. About 45,000 students at 433 secondary schools participated in the 1999 study. The 1999 results indicate that alcohol use among teens has been fairly stable over the past several years. 24 percent of eighth graders, 40 percent of tenth graders, and 51 percent of twelfth graders reported any alcohol consumption in the month prior to the survey.

The National Household Survey on Drug Abuse results

The 1998 survey sample consisted of 25,500 individuals. The household interview takes an average of one hour to complete and uses self-administered answer sheets for the most sensitive portions of the interview. Estimates of the prevalence of alcohol use are defined as follows:

Current use — at least one drink in the past month.

Binge use — five or more drinks on the same occasion at least once in the past month.

Heavy use — five or more drinks on the same occassion on at least five different days in the past month.

According to the 1998 survey, about 10.4 million current drinkers were between 12 and 20 years old in 1998. Of these, 5.1 million were binge drinkers, including 2.3 million heavy drinkers. The rates of current, binge, and heavy alcohol use among the 12 to 20 year old population did not change significantly between 1994 and 1998. Rates in 1998 were 30.6 percent, 15.2 percent, and 6.9 percent, respectively, for current, binge, and heavy use. The rates of binge and heavy alcohol use among young adults ages 18 to 25 were significantly higher in 1998 than in 1997, but similar in 1998 to the rates observed in 1996.

Drinking on campus

Reports of alcohol-related tragedies on college campuses within the last few years have increased the concern of college administrators and parents. Studies show that there has been a decline in drinking in American society as a whole, but recent research has not shown a proportionate decline in drinking among America's college students. You will get many differrent opinions about the abuse of alcohol on college campuses, depending on who you ask, and what their definition of abuse is. Many students do not believe that binge drinking and heavy drinking are alcohol abuse, because they feel it is a normal part of the college experience.

Researchers report that nearly half of all college students are binge drinkers. A 1993 Harvard School of Public Health study of more than 17,000 students indicated that 44 percent had engaged in binge drinking. The study defined binge drinking as five drinks in a row within a short time period for men, and four drinks in a row in a short time period for women. Binge drinking may result in alcohol poisoning, a medical emergency that requires immediate attention. As many as 360,000 of the nation's 12 million undergraduates will die from alcohol-related causes while in school. This is more than the number who will go on to receive M.A. and Ph.D. degrees.

Binge drinking is not just a concern for parents with students at college. Many teens report binge drinking as well. In 1998, 30 percent of the twelfth graders in one survey claimed to have been binge drinking, which was defined as five or more drinks in one sitting, within the previous two weeks.

Health Risks

AIDS, **alcoholism,** alcohol poisoning, cancer, depression and suicide, skin disorders, heart disease, liver disease, and sexually transmitted diseases are all potential consequences of using alcohol. Drinking alcohol affects judgment and relaxes one's sense of social restraint. Risks taken under the influence of alcohol, such as engaging in unprotected sex, expose one's body to infections, diseases, unwanted pregnancy, and acts of violence. Additional and somewhat different health risks are a concern for women because alcohol affects women differently than men. Since women tend to be smaller in size than men are, and their body composition contains more fat, alcohol is absorbed into the body at a faster rate. Women tend to become **addicted** to alcohol more quickly, than men do, and may die younger. Alcohol abuse also plays a significant role in the occurrence of date rape. About 55 percent of female students and 75 percent of male students involved in acquaintance, or date rape, had been drinking or using drugs at the time. With each additional drink, a woman's chance of developing breast cancer, heart disease, and other health problems increases significantly.

Legal Issues

Although alcohol is an illegal **drug** for anyone under the age of 21, laws for DWI vary from state-to-state. Different states have different penalties for people who are caught driving while **intoxicated.** Different states also have different **blood alcohol content** limits. This chart shows the different DWI regulations in each state.

State	BAC	License Suspension first offense	Forfeiture of license	State	BAC	License Suspension first offense	Forfeiture of license
AL	0.08	90 days	no	NE	0.10	90 days	no
AK	0.10	90 days	yes	NV	0.10	90 days	no
AZ	0.10	90 days	yes	NH	0.08	6 months	no[1]
AR	0.10	120 days	yes[1]	NJ	0.10		no
CA	0.08	4 months	yes[1]	NM	0.08	90 days	no
CO	0.10	3 months	no	NY	0.10	variable	yes[1]
CN	0.10	90 days	no	NC	0.08	10 days	yes
DE	0.10	3 months	no[1]	ND	0.10	91 days	yes[1]
Wash. DC	0.10	90 days	no	OH	0.10	90 days	yes[1]
FL	0.08	6 months	no[1]	OK	0.10	180 days	no
GA	0.10	1 year	yes	OR	0.08	90 days	no[1]
HI	0.08	3 months	no	PA	0.10		yes
ID	0.08	90 days	no	RI	0.10		yes
IL	0.08	3 months	no	SC	0.10		yes
IN	0.10	180 days	no[1]	SD	0.10		no[1]
IA	0.10	180 days	no[1]	TN	0.10		yes
KS	0.08	30 days	no[1]	TX	0.10	60 days	yes
KY	0.10		no	UT	0.08	90 days	no[1]
LA	0.10	90 days	no	VT	0.08	90 days	no
ME	0.08	90 days	no[1]	VA	0.08	7 days	no[1]
MD	0.10	45 days	no[1]	WA	0.10		yes
MA	0.08	90 days	no	WV	0.10	6 months	no
MI	0.10		no	WI	0.10	6 months	yes
MN	0.10	90 days	yes[1]	WY	0.10	90 days	no[1]
MS	0.10	90 days	yes				
MO	0.10	30 days	yes				
MT	0.10		yes[1]				

[1]An offender's vehicle may be impounded, the registration suspended, or the license tags confiscated.

Drinking and driving–
"A life is lost every 33 minutes."

Tragically, thousands of Americans are victims of drunk driving each year. Drunk drivers cause more than 20 percent of the traffic deaths in the United States each year. Use of alcohol remains the leading factor in motor vehicle deaths. According to the National Highway Traffic Safety Administration, about three in every ten Americans will be involved in an alcohol-related crash at some time in their lives. There is no way around the fact that alcohol affects one's coordination and response time. Injuries and deaths caused by drunk driving are one hundred percent preventable.

Zero Tolerance

Schools in the United States are enforcing strict school policies on alcohol and other drugs. Encouraged by the U.S. Department of Education, school boards, and principal associations, most schools have established a zero tolerance attitude for violation of alcohol and other drug policies. Typically, this means no excuses are accepted for the use or possession of alcohol while at school or at a school-sponsored event. Severe punishments, such as a year's suspension or expulsion from school, are not unusual, regardless of any other circumstances surrounding the alleged violation. Many students who violate these school policies find themselves out of school, losing credit, not graduating with their classes, and perhaps losing college scholarships. Because of the harsh and inflexible results, zero tolerance policies have met with mixed reviews from students, parents, school faculties, and administrators.

Healthy Choices

The adolescent years

Life can be miserable at times. A best friend rejects you, a boyfriend or girlfriend decides to end a relationship, or maybe that "special someone" doesn't even realize that you exist. Teachers are piling on the homework, and you just cannot figure out algebra no matter what you do! To top it off, your parents are constantly on your back. "Clean your room." "Watch your little brother." "Would you please put on something decent?" are the only words they seem to say. All this is going on at that same time that you are trying to figure out who and what you really are. Do you realize that means all of your friends are probably going through the same thing, and feeling the same way? It's really tough to be a teenager. You are growing up, but you are not there yet. It's okay to feel angry, underappreciated, scared,

or lonely. You might not like feeling the way that you do, but you are supposed to feel things. Feelings help us determine what we think and do about different situations. They help us to figure out who we are. Ask any adult if they ever feel angry, frightened, or alone. If they're honest with you, they will emphatically say "yes!"

Even so, there are days when you just don't want to feel like you do. So what can you do to cope in a healthy way? The first thing you have to do is believe in yourself! Then you need to understand the reasons why you feel as you do. Next, consider the actions that you can take and the resulting consequences of each one. Thinking positively and thinking up real solutions are critical skills for you to know. It's important to remain calm and to control any anger while you think through your plan. As you reach adulthood, you will find the need to use such skills over and over again in your personal life, in school, and in your career. Remember, too, that it's all right to share your feelings and problems with others. Ask for support from a family member, teacher, or friend. You never have to work out your problems all by yourself.

Living a healthy life

As you live your life, do so in a healthy manner. Believe it or not, things like exercise and eating habits really do have a significant impact on your abilities to handle day-to-day stresses. Besides, they help you to look and feel your best. Learn how to relax and how to accept things that you cannot change. Resist the pressure to drink alcohol. Pursue physical fitness instead. Choose recreational activities, including parties, where alcohol won't be served. Be able to state your needs and wants, and to say "no" respectfully. Be prepared to give a reason for your choice not to drink. When you explain your reasons for not wanting to drink, people will respect your decision to say no to alcohol.

Information and Advice

AI-ANON/ALATEEN Family Group

P.O. Box 862
Midtown Station
New York, NY 10018-0862
212-302-7240
800-334-2666 (US)
800-443-4525 (Canada)

AL-ANON / ALATEEN is an organization that offers a support program for families and friends of alcoholics whether or not the alcoholic ever seeks treatment. Members share experiences, and help one another maintain their self-confidence as they cope with the **alcoholism** of someone close to them.

Alcoholics Anonymous

World Service Office
475 Riverside Drive
New York, NY 10115
212-870-3400

Alcoholics Anonymous is an organization that offers alcoholics an opportunity to free themselves of any dependence on alcohol. People in the program must work through twelve steps, improving their self-confidence as they pass each step, until they no longer need alcohol to function.

Center for Science in the Public Interest

1875 Connecticut Avenue, NW,
Suite 300 Washington, DC 20009
phone (202) 332-9110,
fax (202) 265-4954
e-mail cspi@cspinet.org

Center for Science in the Public Interest is a nonprofit association that teaches government officials and the public about nutrition and food safety. They maintain a database of new research results about alcohol called "Booze News."

Children of Alcoholics Foundation, Inc.

P.O. Box 4185
Grand Central Station
New York, NY 10163-4185
800-359-COAF

Children of Alcoholics Foundation is a nonprofit association that provides educational materials and counseling for children and adult children of alcoholics so that they will not abuse alcohol.

Mothers Against Drunk Driving (MADD)

511 East John Carpenter Freeway
Suite 700
Irving, TX 75062
800-GET-MADD

Mothers Against Drunk Driving (MADD) is a nonprofit association made up of volunteers who want to stop drunk driving and underage drinking, and support the victims of drunk driving accidents. To do this the group sponsors public awareness programs like the Designate a Driver program and the Tie One On for Safety campaign.

National Association for Children of Alcoholics

11426 Rickville Pike, Suite 100
Rockville, MD 20852
301-468-0985

The National Association for Children of Alcoholics works to make the public aware of the problems children of alcoholics are faced with. It maintains prevention hotlines and education services, and tries to influence political decisions on topics related to children who come in contact with alcoholism.

National Clearinghouse for Alcohol and Drug Information

P.O. Box 2345
Rockville, MD 208847-2345
800-729-6686

The National Clearinghouse for Alcohol and Drug Information is the largest resource for current information and materials on alcohol and drug abuse. It sends out inexpensive fact sheets, brochures, posters, and videotapes to teach people about alcohol and drugs, and provides counselors, parents, teachers, and community leaders with prevention and treatment materials. In addition, the clearinghouse provides grants for studies of alcohol and drug use, and for various treatment and prevention programs.

National Families in Action (NFIA)

2296 Henderson Mill Road
Suite 300
Atlanta, GA 30345
404-934-6364

National Families in Action is a drug education and prevention group. It works to prevent drug use, abuse, **addiction,** and death, and serves as a messenger between science and the public and then with the law.

National Institute on Alcohol Abuse and Alcoholism (NIAAA)

6000 Executive Boulevard
Willco Building
Bethesda, Maryland 20892-7003

The National Institute on Alcohol Abuse and Alcoholism conducts research on the causes, consequences, and treatment of alcoholism and alcohol-related problems. This group also conducts national and community surveys to determine the risks to alcoholics and underage drinkers, and to discover how many alcoholics there are.

Partnership for a Drug-Free America

405 Lexington Avenue, 16th Floor
New York, New York 10174
(212) 922-1560

The Partnership for a Drug-Free America is a nonprofit association made up of people who work in communications. They produce TV and radio commercials that encourage people to stay away from drugs and alcohol, and run a website with reliable current information on drugs and alcohol.

Schools Without Drugs

U.S. Department of Education
400 Maryland Avenue, SW
Washington, DC 20202
800-624-0100

Schools Without Drugs is an organization that publishes literature about the harmful effects of drug and alcohol use. Two of their most popular books are *The Parent's Guide to Drug Prevention* and *Schools Without Drugs*.

The National Center on Addiction and Substance Abuse at Columbia University

19th floor
633 Third Avenue
New York, NY 10017-6706

The National Center on Addiction and Substance Abuse at Columbia University is an organization that tries to educate the public about what addiction is and how to treat people who are addicted to substances. They want people to know that addiction is a disease, and that it can be treated, and they encourage people to take personal responsibility for their substance abuse and addiction in order to treat it.

Glossary

addiction	compulsive physical and psychological need for a habit forming substance, such as with alcohol
alcoholism	chronic and progressive disease that can be fatal, characterized by continuous or periodic impaired control over drinking
black outs	type of short-term amnesia that an alcoholic may experience
blood alcohol content	measured amount of alcohol in the bloodstream
bootlegger	person who manufactured, sold, or transported alcohol during Prohibition in the United States, 1920–1933
central nervous system	body system pertaining to the brain and spinal cord
chemical dependency	needing to take a substance into the body so badly that one cannot function without it
cope	to deal with and attempt to overcome problems and difficulties
denial	psychological defense mechanism in which a person avoids a problem by refusing to admit that the problem exists
depressant	substance that slows down normal bodily functions and abilities
distillation	chemical process of making alcohol
drug	any substance other than food that affects the way the mind and body work
ethanol	clear unstable liquid made up of carbon, oxygen, and hydrogen
ethnicity	of or relating to large groups of people classed according to common racial, national, religious, or cultural origin or background
euphoria	feeling of excitement, happiness, and well-being
fermentation	slow chemical change that turns one substance into another; most alcoholic beverages are made when yeast converts sugars in grain, or fruit, into alcohol

Fetal Alcohol Syndrome	irreversible physical and mental damage to an unborn child resulting in mental retardation, physical impairements, and facial or skull abnormalities
fetus	unborn human from about three months after conception until birth
gastrointestinal	relating to the stomach or intestines
inhibition	belief, feeling, fear, or other force within a person that keeps that person from acting or thinking freely
intoxication	condition of being drunk
National Prohibition Act	Eighteenth Ammendment to the U.S. Constitution in 1920 that made it illegal to sell or transport alcohol
recovery	treatment and maintenance of an alcoholic to remain sober
risk factors	characteristics associated with a significant likelihood of developing specific problems
Temperance Movement	primarily a religious movement that maintained that alcohol contributed to sinful behavior and break down of families
tolerance	ability of the body to withstand the action of or to become less responsive to a drug

More Books to Read

Haughton, Emma. *Alcohol.* Austin, Tex.: Raintree Steck-Vaughn, 1999.

Miller, Andrew. *Alcohol and Your Liver: The Incredibly Disgusting Story.* New York: Rosen Publishing Group, 2000.

Monroe, Judy. *Alcohol.* Berkeley Heights, N.J.: Enslow Publishers, Inc., 1994.

Ruiz, Ruth Anne. *The Dangers of Binge Drinking.* New York: Rosen Publishing Group, 2000.

Taylor, Barbara. *Everything You Need to Know About Alcohol.* New York: Rosen Publishing Group, 1999.

Index